IN A PEOPLE HOUSE

™ & © Dr. Seuss Enterprises, L.P. All rights reserved

Copyright © 1972 by Dr. Seuss Enterprises, L.P.
All rights reserved
Published by arrangement with Random House Inc.,
New York, USA

First published in the United Kingdom in 1973
This paperback edition published in the United Kingdom by HarperCollins *Children's Books* in 2023
HarperCollins *Children's Books* is a division of HarperCollins*Publishers* Ltd
1 London Bridge Street
London SE1 9GF

www.harpercollins.co.uk

Harper Ireland
Macken House, 39/40 Mayor Street Upper,
Dublin 1, D01 C9W8

1 3 5 7 9 10 8 6 4 2

978-0-00-859295-0

A CIP catalogue record for this title is available from the British Library.

Printed and bound in India

IN A
PEOPLE
HOUSE

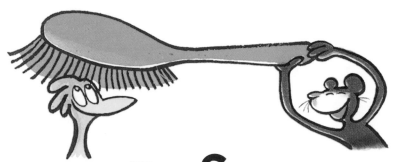

Dr. Seuss
writing as **Theo. LeSieg**

Illustrated by **Roy McKie**

HarperCollins *Children's Books*

"Come inside, Mr. Bird,"
said the mouse.
"I'll show you what there is
in a People House . . .

A People House
has things like . . .

. . . chairs

things like

roller skates

and stairs.

banana

bathtub

bottles

brooms

That's what you find
in people's rooms.

cup
and
saucer

pillow

bed

These are doughnuts.

Here's
a
door.

Come along, I'll show you more.

Here's a
ceiling

here's a floor.

piano

peanuts

popcorn

pails

pencil

paper

hammer

nails

salt and pepper

goldfish

key

table

telephone

TV

Come on!
Come on!
There's more to see!

You'll see a
kitchen sink
in a People House,

a shoe

and a sock

and a clock

said the mouse.

bread **and** butter

window

wall

toothbrush

hairbrush

big blue ball

baked beans

bureau drawers

and

books

lights and lamps

and hats and hooks

mirror

marbles

shirt

and string

knife

fork

spoon

and

bells

to

ring

doll

and

dishes

teapot

trash

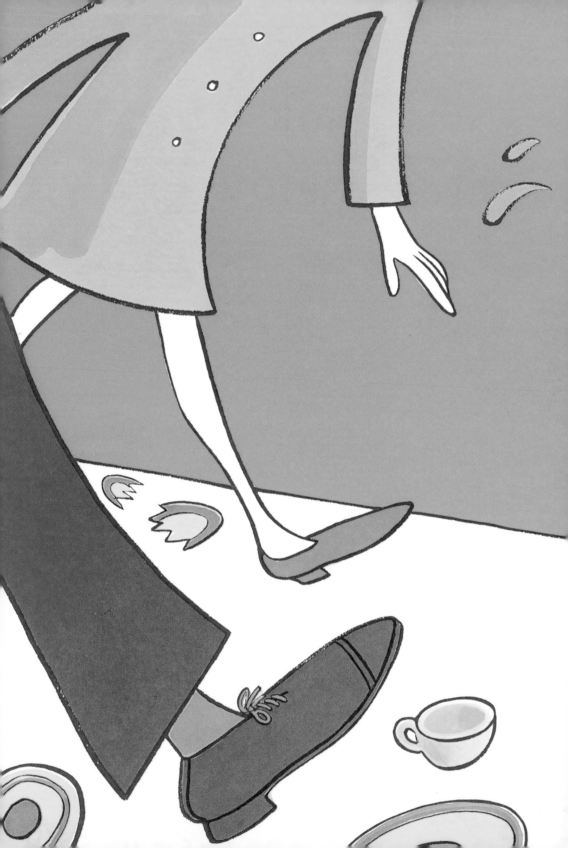

And . . .
Another thing,
it's time
you knew . . .

. . . A People House

has people, too!

"And now, Mr. Bird,
you know," said the mouse.
"You know what there is
in a People House."